Contents

Aisha and Emily are best friends from Spellford Village. Aisha loves sports, whilst Emily's favourite thing is science. But what both girls enjoy more than anything is visiting Enchanted Valley and helping their unicorn friends who live there.

Dawnblaze

Dawnblaze is the Fire Unicorn. She loves to swim in the hot springs on Firework Mountain with her dragon friends!

The Air Unicorn, Shimmerbreeze, is in charge of making sure the air in Enchanted Valley is fresh and clean. She likes to use her magic to create little breezes, so her friends can fly their kites.

Shimmerbreeze

Glitterhoof

Glitterhoof is the Earth Unicorn, who makes plants grow strong and beautiful. What she likes best is being part of a team – there's nothing she won't do for her friends!

Sparklesplash has so much fun playing in the rivers and lagoons of Enchanted Valley. This Water Unicorn wants everyone to love the water, just as much as she does.

Sparklesplash

Enchanted Cottage

Golden Palace

An Enchanted Valley lies a twinkle away,
Where beautiful unicorns live, laugh and play
You can visit the mermaids, or go for a ride,
So much fun to be had, but dangers can hide!

Your friends need your help ~ this is how you know:
A keyring lights up with a magical glow.
Whirled off like a dream, you won't want to leave.
Friendship forever, when you truly believe.

Chapter One
Trouble in Enchanted Valley

Aisha Khan pointed up at the sky.
"Look!" she said with a grin. "There's an
elephant!"

Aisha and her best friend, Emily Turner,
were lying on the lawn of Enchanted
Cottage, watching the fluffy clouds float
past – and spotting the ones shaped

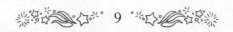

like animals! Aisha and her parents had moved to Spellford Village just a few days ago, and the two girls were already close. Together they had explored Aisha's new home, Enchanted Cottage – and discovered that the old thatched house held a wonderful secret …

"Aren't the clouds pretty?" said Emily. "Did you know that they're made of tiny droplets of water?" Emily loved science, just as much as Aisha loved sport.

"Cool!" said Aisha. Then she gasped. "Look at that one!" She pointed to where a large cloud was drifting over the top of the phoenix statue in the middle of the lawn. The cloud had a long tail and neck, and two great wings. It seemed to be pointing its tail down towards the outstretched wings of the magic bird below.

"Wow!" said Emily. "It's a dragon cloud!"

The girls shared an excited grin. On Aisha's first day in Spellford, they had found a beautiful crystal model of a unicorn in the attic of Enchanted Cottage. When a sunbeam had touched the glittering model, they'd been transported to Enchanted Valley, a wonderful kingdom ruled over by friendly flying unicorns, and full of other magical creatures, too – like goblins and dragons!

"I can't wait to visit the unicorns again," said Aisha with a sigh. She took out a crystal unicorn keyring from her shorts pocket. Queen Aurora, the unicorn ruler of the valley, had given matching keyrings to the girls and promised they'd return to Enchanted Valley very soon. Emily took her keyring out of her jeans pocket too.

Suddenly, the dragon cloud seemed to shimmer, then melted away – letting a beam of sunlight shine down on the girls. Their keyrings began to glow and sparkle like magical stars.

Both girls leaped
to their feet. "Is
Queen Aurora
calling us?" Aisha
asked, excitement
racing through her.

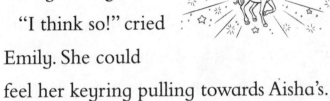

"I think so!" cried
Emily. She could
feel her keyring pulling towards Aisha's.
"Whoa! They're like magnets!"

"Let's try putting them together," said
Aisha.

The girls held the two tiny unicorns so
that their horns touched. The keyrings
glowed, with every colour of the rainbow
swirling inside them. Then, suddenly, there

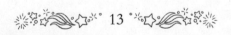

was an explosion of light like dazzling fireworks. Emily and Aisha felt their feet lift off the grass.

In a whirl of sparkles, the garden and Enchanted Cottage vanished. Bright swirls of colour whizzed around them, and they were lifted up, up, up ...

A few moments later, the girls drifted to the ground once more and the sparkles cleared. They found themselves at the foot of a hill, on which stood a dazzling gold palace.

"We're back in Enchanted Valley!" cried Aisha, turning a cartwheel in delight.

Laughing, the girls held hands and walked up the hill to the palace.

Sweet-scented flowers grew over the palace walls, and twirling turrets, like upside-down ice cream cones, rose in the air. A river wound magically up from the sea to fill the moat – when the girls

looked down over the valley, they could
follow its path as it babbled through
green meadows, forests and lakes.

"It's so amazing to be here again!" said
Emily, with a sigh of happiness.

The palace's silver drawbridge lowered
and a beautiful unicorn wearing a
gleaming crown trotted out. Her coat

shone with all the
shades of sunrise –
from bright yellows
to rich reds and
fiery oranges. Her
horn was long
and elegant and
gleamed in the
sunshine.

"Queen Aurora!" The girls threw their arms around her soft neck in a tight hug.

Aurora laughed, the sound as beautiful as a flute's music. "Welcome, girls!" she said. "It's so lovely to see you." But then her eyes clouded with worry.

"What's the matter?" asked Emily.

"Come and see," said Aurora sadly.

She took them across the drawbridge and into a courtyard, past a fountain shaped like a leaping dolphin to where a pink-and-white stripy tent stood on a lawn. Beside it were the four Nature Unicorns!

"Hello!" cried the girls, hugging them each in turn.

"Hello, girls," said Dawnblaze the fire

unicorn, whose coat was red. "Oh, thank goodness you're here!"

"We need your help," said Sparklesplash the water unicorn, who was a shimmering blue. "Look!"

With her horn, Sparklesplash pointed at a heap of brightly coloured kites lying at the unicorns' hooves.

"We're hoping to have a kite-flying competition at the Nature Gala," said Glitterhoof the earth unicorn, who was a pretty shade of leaf green.

"But the kites won't leave the ground," added Dawnblaze.

Shimmerbreeze the air unicorn gave a sad sigh. Her coat was as white as snow and her mane and tail were a glittery silver. Her pale blue eyes were wet with tears. "It's because my locket is missing," she said.

All the unicorns of Enchanted Valley wore crystal lockets around their necks that gave them magical powers.

Queen Aurora's locket contained two tiny
suns, dancing happily around each other
like friends playing – and she looked after
friendship in the valley. But out of the
four Nature Unicorns, only Dawnblaze
was wearing a locket now. The others had
been stolen by a wicked unicorn called
Selena, who would stop at nothing to rule
over Enchanted Valley.

Emily and Aisha had managed to get

Dawnblaze's locket back from Selena's horrible clutches, but it had been very difficult.

Queen Aurora turned to the girls. "This is why I've brought you to Enchanted Valley today," she said. Her eyes were wide and serious. "I'm worried that the kites are just the start of the trouble Selena will cause with Shimmerbreeze's locket. We need your help to get it back."

"We'd do anything to save the valley," said Aisha.

"Of course we will!" promised Emily.

Just then, the courtyard darkened, and they all looked up. A mysterious blanket of grey cloud was drifting over the palace, blocking out the sun. The air grew

thick and dusty, making everyone cough
and splutter.

"Yuck!" said Aisha. "The air's turned so
dirty!"

"What's happening?" asked Emily,
between coughs.

Then shrill
laughter filled
their ears – and
the girls knew
exactly who
was behind the
nasty, dirty fog.
A silver unicorn
with a twilight-
blue mane burst
from the filthy

cloud, bolts of electricity flashing from her horn.

"Uh-oh," said Emily and Aisha. "It's Selena!"

Chapter Two
The Terrible Tornado

Selena landed in the courtyard in front of the horrified girls and unicorns. Her purple eyes blazed and her mane and tail bristled. She reared up, her hooves flashing. Inside her locket were tiny storm clouds, zigzags of jagged lightning crackling through them.

"So you snivelling girls are back,"
Selena sneered.

Swallowing down their fear, Emily and
Aisha stood their ground.

"That's right," said Aisha firmly. "The
unicorns are our friends, and friends help
each other."

"Two little squirts like you won't stop
me becoming queen of Enchanted
Valley," spat Selena, swishing her dark

blue tail menacingly.

A giggle came from the dirty cloud, and down flapped Flit, Selena's naughty bat servant. "Hee, hee!" laughed Flit. "They're little squirts and you're going to be queen! You tell them, Your Silver Greatness!"

"I just did, Flit!" screeched Selena. "Hand over the crown, Aurora!"

"You will never be queen," said Aurora firmly.

"We'll see about that!" Selena stamped her hooves. "The power of the air locket is mine now – and it's hidden where you'll never find it. If you don't make me queen, the air will get dirtier and dirtier, until

Enchanted Valley is covered in my
yucky-mucky fog!"

A bolt of lightning shot from her horn.
The filthy cloud began whirl around,
sucking up petals and leaves from the
garden.

"Oh no!" gasped Queen Aurora.
"Selena's creating a–a—"

"A tornado!" finished Emily.

The tornado spun faster and faster. It
pulled up the kites, then a whole rose

bush, like a gigantic vacuum cleaner.
Then the girls and the unicorns were
being tugged upwards – their hair, manes
and tails were standing on end. The
unicorns' hooves were still on the ground,
but the girls were smaller and lighter, and
the tornado pulled them up on to their
tiptoes. "Whoa!" they both cried, as they
were lifted off the ground.

Tumbling, whirling wind blasted around
them. Dust stung their eyes and they

felt horribly dizzy as they were swept higher and higher. Below, they saw Shimmerbreeze take off, but before she could get close enough to the girls to save them, she was sucked up into the tornado, too!

Soon, the palace and their unicorn friends had vanished from sight. Emily, Aisha and Shimmerbreeze were tossed helplessly about in the fierce wind as the tornado flew across Enchanted Valley. It hoovered up fir cones, twigs and stones, umbrellas and garden spades. Even a washing line full of tiny, flapping gnome clothes spun by in a swirling rush.

Emily shrieked as a flying sock whipped against her face.

A pebble hit Aisha on the arm. "Ow!" she yelped.

Then, as quickly as it had started, the tornado stopped spinning. The air became perfectly still. For a long moment, the girls, Shimmerbreeze and all the different objects floated high above the clouds. Then they began to plummet!

Terrified, the girls grabbed each other's hands. Down and down they fell, twisting and turning.

"Help!" screamed Emily.

Shimmerbreeze gave a whinny of alarm. "I'll save you!" she called.

She dived after the girls as they tumbled through the air, their hearts hammering with fright.

"Please hurry, Shimmerbreeze!" Aisha cried.

But Shimmerbreeze was fighting her way through the leaves and clothes and old umbrellas also falling to the ground.

"They're slowing her down!" shouted Emily. Then she spotted something else flying through the sky – a brilliant flash of red and gold, hurtling towards the girls like a rocket. When it got closer, they realised it was a beautiful giant bird.

The bird shot beneath the girls – and

they landed on her soft feathered back.

"Hold tight!" the bird squawked. She had a crest of orange feathers on her head and a long glossy tail that fanned out like flames. The girls clung on as they flew down towards a fluffy cloud. To their astonishment, the bird came to rest on top of it! She neatly folded her huge wings.

"We're safe!" breathed Aisha.

"Thank you for catching us!" said Emily.

"Don't mention it, my dears," chirruped

the kindly bird.

Shimmerbreeze landed next to them, shaking a pair of gnome trousers from her horn. "I'm so glad you're all right," she said, nuzzling their cheeks. "Thank you for your help," she said to the bird. Then she turned to the girls. "This is Ember. She's a phoenix."

Emily and Aisha grinned. They loved the phoenix statue in the garden of Enchanted Cottage. They'd never dreamed they'd meet one in real life!

"It's nice to meet you, Ember," said Aisha.

"Welcome to my cloud," the phoenix said. "Off you hop!"

The girls looked doubtfully at the cloud.

Shimmerbreeze and Ember might be able to stand on it, but they were magic! What if the girls fell straight through?

"It's quite safe," Shimmerbreeze assured them.

The girls climbed carefully off Ember's back. They felt their feet sink just a little into the fluffy surface. It was like stepping on to a soft cushion.

"This is amazing!" exclaimed Emily, looking at the wisps curling around her

Aisha jumped up and down, springing higher than Emily's head. "It's like a trampoline!" she cried, and turned a backflip.

Ember laughed in delight. "I do enjoy having visitors," she said, rustling the long feathers of her tail. "Especially today! My eggs have started to sing, which means it won't be long until they hatch!"

Emily and Aisha grinned at each other. Bouncy clouds and singing eggs! Enchanted Valley was full of amazing surprises!

Ember led them to a billowy white nest in the middle of the cloud. Six sparkling gold eggs lay snugly inside. And they were singing, in tiny, trilling voices!

Fluffy clouds that bob along
Listen to our happy song.
We're floating gently way up high
Warm and comfy in the sky.

"How sweet!" said Emily. "In Aisha's garden there's a—"

Her words were lost in a howling noise that filled the air. A whirling column raced above the clouds.

"The tornado's back!" cried Shimmerbreeze.

Swoosh! The girls watched in horror as the tornado whizzed through the sky above them. They clung tightly to Shimmerbreeze to keep from being swept up this time – but before anyone could reach it, the nest shot up into the sky.

"No!" yelled Aisha, and bounced up from the cloud. She tried to snatch the nest back, but it spiralled higher and higher in the spinning cone of wind.

With a whoosh, the tornado whisked
the precious eggs away!

Chapter Three
A Fluffy Surprise

"My chicks!" cried Ember, squawking with panic.

She took off and chased after the tornado, her flame-coloured wings flapping in a blur.

"We have to help her," said Emily.

"Jump on, girls," said Shimmerbreeze.

Aisha climbed on to her back, Emily
behind her. Shimmerbreeze cantered
across the cloud, wisps swirling around
her hooves, then leaped into the air.
Although they were on a rescue mission,
the girls couldn't help feeling a rush
of excitement – they were flying on a
unicorn!

Shimmerbreeze sped through the sky,
catching up with Ember. The phoenix's
eyes were fixed on her precious nest,
which was spinning around in the wind.

But the air was turning mucky and gloopy with dirt, slowing them down. The tornado was speeding away.

"It's just ... so hard ... to ... fly!" Shimmerbreeze panted. The tornado sped off into the distance until it was just a grubby dot on the horizon. Then it was gone.

"No!" cried Aisha.

"My chicks will be hatching any minute," wailed Ember. "They'll be all alone." She flopped on to a nearby cloud. "Oh, look at that!" She pointed a wing to the edge of the cloud, which the dirty air was turning a sludgy green. "And when they hatch, they'll be surrounded by this horrible dirt! The poor things!" She hid

her head in her wings.

Shimmerbreeze landed beside her and the girls jumped down. They stroked Ember's feathers gently.

Emily shared a glance with Aisha. She knew her friend was thinking the same thing – they needed to look for Shimmerbreeze's locket to stop the air getting even dirtier, but they couldn't leave the poor phoenix. "We'll get your eggs back," Emily told her.

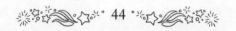

"The tornado put us down earlier," said Aisha, "so maybe it's put the nest down too. Let's search the clouds for it."

"What a good idea," said Ember, wiping her eyes with a wingtip. "It's so kind of you to help."

"Follow me!" said Aisha. Using the cloud as a trampoline once more, she bounced on to the next one. Emily bounced after her, while Ember and Shimmerbreeze flew around, searching anxiously. They went from cloud to cloud, each now so tinged with dirt they looked more like puffs of smoke from a fire. The phoenix's nest was nowhere to be seen.

Ember coughed on the filthy air. "It's no good," she said sadly.

"Wait!" cried Shimmerbreeze. "Can you hear that?"

From somewhere nearby came a strange, sad whimpering sound.

"Is it the eggs singing?" asked Aisha.

Ember cocked her head to listen. "I don't think so," she said.

"It's someone crying," said Emily.

"Where's it coming from?" asked Aisha, puzzled.

"Oh, boo hoo! Boo hoo hoo!" went the crying sound. It was getting louder. The cloud the girls were standing on started to shake.

"Hang on tight!" squawked Ember. "It's another tornado!"

"Jump on my back!" cried

Shimmerbreeze.

Before the girls could move, the front of the cloud began to shift and grow, and suddenly became an enormous white furry head. It turned slowly towards them and blinked its big, wet eyes. The girls saw that it had two soft floppy ears, a round, shiny nose and wispy white whiskers. Emily and Aisha were open-mouthed in amazement. They weren't standing on a cloud – they were on a creature!

"He's a cloud puppy," whispered Shimmerbreeze.

"He's adorable!" breathed Emily.

"Hello," said the cloud puppy, sniffling softly. "My name is Fluffy."

"Hello, Fluffy," said Aisha. She leaned

forward and stroked his ears, giggling as his whiskers tickled her face. "I'm Aisha and this is Emily, and Shimmerbreeze, and Ember …"

She stopped. Tears as big as footballs were rolling down the puppy's face.

"Why are you sad, Fluffy?" asked Emily anxiously.

"A horrid tornado stole my golden

ball," sniffed the cloud puppy. "It's my favourite one to play fetch with." He gave a mournful howl that made him tremble all over. The girls held hands so they wouldn't fall from his back.

"The tornado stole Ember's eggs, too," said Emily. "You haven't seen them, have you?"

"No!" wailed Fluffy, crying even harder.

"This is all because horrible Selena stole Shimmerbreeze's locket," explained Aisha. "It's why the air's so dirty. We're on a quest to find the locket, and we'll find your ball too."

Fluffy stopped crying. His tail wagged.

"Thank you," he said, and barked cheerfully. "Can I help too?"

"Of course you can," said Aisha.

Emily peered thoughtfully through the murky air. "Let's all fly higher," she said, "then we might spot where the tornado's gone."

"Hold on tight," said Fluffy, "and off we go!"

The girls rode on Fluffy's back while Shimmerbreeze and Ember soared beside them. Up they zoomed through the sky. Swirls of murky air billowed

around, making it hard to see. Below the clouds, the usually fresh green forests and sparkling lakes of Enchanted Valley had turned grey and sludgy.

"Everywhere is so miserable," said Emily sadly, gazing down at the horrible sight.

Fluffy gave a whine. "What's that down there?" he asked. "It looks horrible!"

Aisha followed his gaze – and saw a dark smudge skidding across one of the meadows. "It's the tornado!"

"Well spotted, Fluffy!" cried
Shimmerbreeze.

"Chase it, Fluffy!" called Emily.
"Hurry!"

Chapter Four
Hob Helps Out

Fluffy, Shimmerbreeze and Ember
swooped down after the twisting tornado.
Emily and Aisha clung on to Fluffy's fur
as they rushed towards the ground. The
tornado whirled over the fields towards
what looked like an enormous rubbish
heap. The tornado spun over the heap,

dropping all the things it had stolen. The whole mound was covered in grime, and blasts of filthy dust burst from its centre.

"The tornado's making a rubbish dump!" squawked Ember in horror.

A shudder rippled through Shimmerbreeze's coat. "I've never seen anything so filthy before!"

"It's the dirtiest place in Enchanted Valley," agreed Fluffy.

Emily frowned, thinking hard. Fluffy's words had given her an idea … "We know from when we found Dawnblaze's locket that Selena's horrible magic comes from the locket," she said. "So wherever the locket is, it will be making everything around it dirty. Even dirtier than here …"

"...So if the rubbish heap is the dirtiest place in Enchanted Valley," finished Aisha, "that must be where the locket is!"

They waited until the tornado had whirled away again, then landed beside the pile of rubbish. But as soon as they approached the dump, the dust made them all start coughing.

"This is no good," spluttered Aisha. "We can't go any closer."

"I know!" exclaimed Emily. "If I'm doing science experiments, I always wear a mask. It stops me breathing in anything bad." She frowned. "But where can we find masks in Enchanted Valley?"

Aisha's eyes lit up. "I know! Hob!"

Hob the little goblin was a very talented

potion maker. On their first adventure, the girls had helped him make a magic potion to warm up the dragons of Firework Mountain. "I bet he wears a mask when he's making his potions," Aisha said.

"His cave isn't far from here," said Shimmerbreeze eagerly.

"I'd love to take you," said Fluffy, "but I have to get away from here." He gave himself a shake and a shower of dirt fell from his coat. "Soon I'll be so grubby, I'll be too heavy to fly!"

"You've been really helpful already," said Aisha, stroking his soft head. "You spotted the tornado!"

"I'll carry the girls," Shimmerbreeze

told the cloud puppy.

"We won't forget your ball, Fluffy,"
Emily assured him.

She climbed on to Shimmerbreeze's
silky back behind her friend.

"Goodbye," called Fluffy, waving a big,
soft paw. "And good luck."

Shimmerbreeze took off, with Ember
close behind. The air was growing thicker
every minute, full of grit and flying
objects – picnic baskets and tiny bicycles

swept past them towards the rubbish
heap. The girls covered their mouths and
ducked and darted to avoid getting hit,
but their throats were becoming sore.
As Shimmerbreeze battled through the
grimy mist they thought they could
hear awful coughing coming from every
corner of Enchanted Valley.

Finally, Shimmerbreeze dived towards a
forest at the foot of Firework Mountain.

As they dipped
below the trees,
they saw an old,
stooped goblin in a
long purple gown
and pointed hat. He
was trying to sweep
away the grime

piling up at the entrance to his cave.

"Poor Hob!" gasped Aisha. "This nasty
dust is spoiling his lovely home."

Hob dropped his broom as
Shimmerbreeze and the girls landed
nearby. Ember flapped down with a
friendly squawk.

"What a lovely surprise!" Hob
exclaimed, taking off his gold spectacles

to wipe them free of dust. "Come in, everyone, come in." Then a frown spread over his green, wrinkly face. "Mind where you walk. This horrible dust has made my garden very dirty. And just a few minutes ago, a terrible wind nearly swept me away! It pulled my best silver pruning scissors straight from my hands."

"It's not just here," Emily told him. "Selena is ruining the whole of Enchanted Valley." She and Aisha quickly explained what was happening.

"So we have to find Shimmerbreeze's locket," Aisha said. "But it's hard to breathe in this horrid air. Do you have any masks we could use?"

Hob nodded. They followed him inside,

down a dark, winding tunnel into a big cavern, which glowed silver and gold from the light of sparkling crystals and lanterns. Wonky shelves had been wedged between the rocks. They were full of thick books, and colourful potions in old bottles. Each bottle was labelled with neat writing – *Thistle dewdrops*, *Wiggly woodbine*, *Midnight rosebuds* and many more.

Hob pulled four white masks out from a set of rickety drawers.

"They look just right!" said Shimmerbreeze.

"They won't be enough on

their own," said Hob, tapping his finger to his mouth. "This air is so filthy we need a fresh air potion." He scuttled round, peering at the shelves. "Would you help me, girls? You were such wonderful assistants last time you were here."

"Of course," chorused Emily and Aisha.

"Excellent!" The little goblin rubbed his gnarly hands together. "First I need a teaspoon of sweetmeadow water." He pointed up to the highest corner of the cavern.

In a flash, Aisha had climbed up a narrow ladder to a high shelf and pulled down a green jar. "Found it," she said, handing it down to Emily.

"Next it's ten moonflower petals," said

Hob, "then three sugar-apples and a sprig of windgrass."

When they'd fetched all the ingredients, Hob put each in turn into a blackened pot on the fire. He slowly stirred the mixture with a wooden spoon nearly as tall and gnarled as he was. Now and then, he sniffed at it.

Soon a wonderful smell of newly cut

grass wafted out of the pot. Hob gave
a final stir and a satisfied bob of his
head. "It's ready," he said with a smile.
He dipped each mask in the purply-
pink mixture. To the girls' surprise, when
the masks came out, they were already
dry. They put them on and helped
Shimmerbreeze and Ember to fasten
theirs. Aisha took a deep breath. The air
in her mask was fresh and cool, like a
dewy spring morning.

"Thank you so much, Hob," said Emily.

"Think nothing of it," said Hob. "I'm
glad to help beat that wicked Selena.
Good luck."

They waved goodbye and made their
way back through the dark passage and

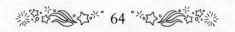

out into the forest.

"How wonderful to be able to breathe properly again!" Aisha said, giggling through her mask. "I feel like I'm breathing the first air of the morning."

"Same here," said Emily.

"And here," said Shimmerbreeze and Ember together.

Shimmerbreeze knelt down so the girls could climb on her back. She sped into

a gallop and then took off towards the
rubbish heap, Ember flying at her side.

"Now let's find that pendant!" said
Aisha.

Chapter Five
Trapped

Even though they could all breathe easily
now, a thick coat of grey dust clung
to Shimmerbreeze's mane and Ember's
feathers, and stuck to the girls' clothes.

"It's so hard to fly," panted
Shimmerbreeze after a while.

"Maybe we should walk the rest of the

way," said Emily. "We must be nearly there by now!"

"Good idea, Emily," Ember squawked.

Shimmerbreeze and Ember battled through the murk to land by a stream that looked as though it were full of dirty treacle. The girls quickly jumped down, sending the dust on their clothes swirling.

The rubbish mound loomed up ahead like a horrible mountain.

"What an awful place," said Aisha. "But

it's not going to beat us. We're going to find Shimmerbreeze's locket."

"And your eggs, Ember," said Emily.

"Thank you, my dears," said Ember gratefully. "And we mustn't forget Fluffy's ball."

Aisha led the way as the group crunched over fallen tree branches and around scattered bits of furniture and clothing. It looked like everyone in Enchanted Valley must have lost

something to the tornado.

As they reached the heap, there was a loud flapping overhead.

They looked up through the clouds of dirt, but saw nothing.

Then Emily shrieked and Aisha pointed up, just as something dark and heavy fell on top of them.

"It's a net!" Aisha cried. "We're trapped!"

The four friends pulled at the rope net, but the more they struggled the more they became tangled up inside it. Something small and black was flying around them, making a familiar chittering sound.

"It's Flit!" gasped Emily.

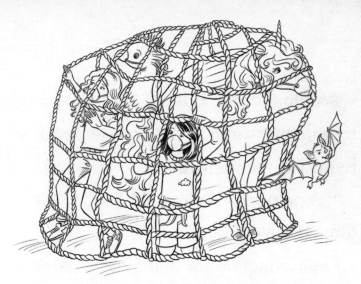

"I'm such a clever bat!" cackled Flit. "I've captured you, and now Selena will think I'm the best sidekick ever. I'll go and tell her, and she can decide what to do with you!" He flew away, screeching with laughter.

"What are we going to do?" squealed Ember. "We'll never get out. My poor eggs!"

"I'm sure there's a way," said Emily. "We've just got to think."

Shimmerbreeze took off her mask and tried to bite through the rope, while Aisha tugged at the net with all her strength.

"It's no good," she panted finally. "It's just getting tighter."

Emily caught sight of a glint of silver on the ground. She gently moved the dirt with her foot and uncovered a little pair of silver scissors.

Aisha gasped. "Hob said the tornado had stolen his scissors," she said. "Those must be his – they can help us escape!"

Emily wriggled in their rope cage until she managed to stretch down and hook her fingers round the scissors handles. She began to cut the net. It was thick and coarse, but Hob's scissors were sharp.

Finally she had cut a girl-sized hole.

"Well done, Emily!" said Shimmerbreeze.

Emily grinned and squeezed her way out. Aisha followed. Then they snipped away more of the net and helped Ember and Shimmerbreeze through the gap.

"What a relief!" said Ember, smoothing down her rumpled feathers.

Shimmerbreeze raised her head. "Can you hear that?" she asked.

Everyone listened. From the distance came a sweet song.

"That's my chicks, singing inside their eggs!" cried Ember.

"But where are they?" asked Aisha, peering through the murk. "I wish it wasn't so dark."

"I can help with that," said Ember. She curled her enormous tail all the way over her head. The tips of the long crimson feathers lit up and glowed like fairy lights.

"Wow!" gasped the girls.

"Follow me!" Ember squawked.

"Wait," said Emily. "We might get lost." She unravelled the net into a long rope and coiled it over her arm. "If we unwind it as we go, we'll be able to find our way back."

She slipped Hob's scissors into her pocket and they followed the phoenix over the rough ground. The wind howled round the rubbish heap as they climbed over piles of lanterns, dusters and garden

spades. Shimmerbreeze's hooves slipped
every now and then, and Aisha and Emily
clutched each other to keep from falling.

The song grew louder. The girls could
make out the words now:

> Fluffy clouds that bob along
> Listen to our happy song.
> Soon we chicks will hatch and fly
> Whizzing round the bright blue sky!

"We must be very close," said Shimmerbreeze.

Ember slowly turned so that the lights on her tail lit up the rubbish all around them.

Everyone looked closely at the grimy mess. There were heaps of books, stacks of teacups, a matching set of velvet armchairs and—

"Look!" exclaimed Aisha, pointing to a downy wisp of white just poking out from a pile of milk jugs. It was a nest made of cloud – with a clutch of golden eggs inside!

"My eggs!" exclaimed Ember, flapping her wings in excitement. Emily and Aisha moved the milk jugs out of the way, and

Ember folded her wings lovingly around her nest. She cooed softly to the chicks inside the gleaming shells.

"They're safe!" breathed Aisha. "You should take them home, Ember. Before they hatch!"

"Aisha's right," said Shimmerbreeze. "The girls and I will stay and find my locket."

The phoenix smiled at her friends, but planted her feet firmly on the ground and lifted her tail up even higher.

"I'm staying too," she said firmly. "You helped me, and now I'll help you defeat that dreadful Selena!"

Chapter Six
Into the Wind

"On with our search," said
Shimmerbreeze. "My locket must be
somewhere in this heap."

Ember picked up her precious nest and
sheltered it under one wing. Her bobbing
lights led them higher and higher up the
rubbish heap, Emily unravelling the rope

behind them as they went. The wind grew fiercer, tearing at the girls' clothes and whipping their hair around their faces.

As they reached the top of the heap, it began to tremble, and Emily gasped. Up ahead, a funnel of wind was spiralling quickly towards them.

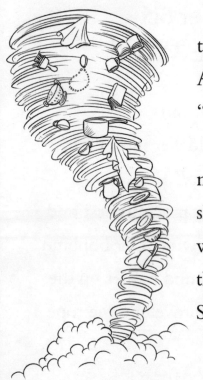

"It's that horrible tornado!" yelled Aisha over the wind. "Bringing more stuff!"

Emily could just make out something shiny tumbling round with all the rubbish in the tornado's winds. She squinted. It was a pendant on a silver chain!

"Look!" she cried.

Shimmerbreeze whinnied in delight –
but then her ears drooped. "How will we
get it back? The tornado will suck us in!"

Emily thought hard. She looked at the
rope she was carrying. It stretched out
behind her but there was plenty still coiled
around her hand. "One of us could go
into the tornado if they have the rope tied
around them, while someone holds the
other end," she said. "Then, when they've
grabbed the locket, we can pull them
back out."

"Sounds fun," said Aisha. "I volunteer
for tornado duty!"

Emily smiled gratefully at Aisha, who

fastened the rope round her waist. Emily
and Shimmerbreeze held the other end
tightly.

"Here I go," yelled Aisha. She leapt into
the rushing wind and felt herself being
lifted high off the ground. "Whoa!" she
shouted as she whizzed around. "I'm like
a human kite!"

All sorts of bits and pieces were flying
round her – forks and paintbrushes
and potted plants. As she dodged the

objects, Aisha could feel that her friends were holding her firmly. The locket was twirling in a dizzying circle, close by. Aisha reached for it, but the locket spun away. She felt the rope go slack and she was pulled deeper into the roaring wind.

"What's happening?" she yelled.

"The rope's slipping through my hands," Emily yelled back. "I can't hold on for much longer!" Aisha felt a flutter of panic.

"I'll help you, Emily!" came Ember's voice.

Aisha could just see the phoenix below her. The brightly coloured bird had grasped the rope in her beak and dug her talons into the ground. To Aisha's relief, the rope went tight once more.

She peered anxiously through the spinning column of wind, looking for the locket. It flashed by just out of reach. It was going too fast! The next time it whirled towards Aisha, she made a desperate lunge. She felt her fingers close over the precious pendant.

"Got it!" she shouted in triumph.

Her three friends gave a great pull and towed her out of the wind.

Aisha looped the chain over Shimmerbreeze's head. Everyone took a deep breath and held it. Could the magic of the locket save Enchanted Valley?

Then, *whoosh!* A tablecloth rose from the rubbish heap and whizzed away. *Whizz!* Cups, saucers and plates followed. One by one, all the objects in the rubbish heap began to fly off. The girls felt themselves slowly sinking back to the ground as the heap shrank.

"What's happening?" asked Emily.

"I think everything's returning to its owners," Ember replied.

"Then Fluffy should have his ball back any minute!" said Emily. Just then, Hob's scissors wriggled out from her pocket and flew off, too.

"The air's cleared!" said Aisha taking off her mask. The others did the same, each taking in a deep breath of the clean, fresh breeze.

The rubbish heap had been hiding a lush green meadow. Dragonflies flittered between pink poppies and delicate yellow buttercups. A gentle wind rustled through the trees and the air was full of birdsong. Enchanted Valley was beautiful once more!

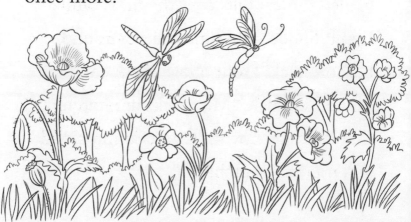

Chapter Seven
Phoenix Chicks

They all cheered in celebration. Aisha
turned somersaults over the grass while
Emily hugged Shimmerbreeze around
her soft neck. From above them came an
excited squawk. "My chicks are hatching,"
Ember called down. "Come to my cloud
and you can watch!"

"Hop on, girls," said Shimmerbreeze.

They didn't need telling twice.
Shimmerbreeze soared swiftly through
the fresh, sweet air towards Ember's cloud.
They could see Enchanted Valley spread
out below. Every speck of rubbish was
gone. Buttery sunbeams shone on its
lush mountains and crystal-clear streams
flowed down the hillsides. Unicorns were
galloping over the green slopes and little

dragons played happily in the water.

They rose higher and higher until Shimmerbreeze landed on Ember's fluffy white cloud. Ember perched next to them and gently put down the nest. The girls jumped off Shimmerbreeze's back and knelt to watch the eggs. The singing had stopped. Now a tapping sound was coming from inside one of them. Emily and Aisha held hands tightly and watched a small crack appear in its shell. A tiny beak poked through. At last a little orange head popped out and gave a merry chirp.

"It's so cute," breathed Aisha.

Ember pulled the shell away with her claw and the baby phoenix waddled about, shaking its bright orange and red feathers. Another egg cracked, and another. Soon there were six adorable little chicks, squealing and hopping all over the cloud. Emily and Aisha stroked their downy heads.

"Thank you, girls," said Ember. "Thank you, Shimmerbreeze. You saved my babies."

"We're so glad we could help," replied Emily.

Then they heard a woof and turned to watch as Fluffy floated down beside them. "You've cleaned up the air," he barked happily. "Did you find my ball?"

Emily and Aisha exchanged a glance.

"Hasn't it flown back to you?" said Aisha, puzzled.

Fluffy's tail drooped and he shook his head sadly.

Just then, Emily spotted something caught in the down of Ember's nest.

"How many eggs did you have,

Ember?" she asked.

"Six, dear," said Ember. "And every one now hatched and happy."

Emily picked up the object from the nest. It was shiny and golden but it wasn't shaped like an egg. It was completely round. Emily smiled.

"I've found your ball, Fluffy!" she called.

The puppy gave a yip of delight and wagged his tail so hard that his whole body wiggled, sending wisps of cloud everywhere.

"Fetch, Fluffy!" Aisha took the ball and threw it high into the sky.

Fluffy gave a joyful bark and dashed off after his beloved toy as the others laughed with pleasure. All was right in Enchanted

Valley once again!

"We should be getting back to the palace," said Shimmerbreeze. "Hop on, girls, for one last ride!"

Emily and Aisha rushed round hugging Ember and kissing the chicks goodbye. Then they jumped on to Shimmerbreeze's back and they were off, soaring over Enchanted Valley while the sweet-smelling wind danced in their hair.

Soon the golden walls of Aurora's palace gleamed in the distance and the

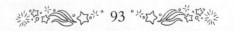

spiral turrets sparkled in the sun's warm rays. In the courtyard, unicorns were busy decorating the walls and hedges with streamers and bunting.

Dawnblaze, Sparklesplash and Glitterhoof stood by the tent, blowing up balloons all the colours of the rainbow.

Shimmerbreeze landed beside them. Aurora galloped out from the tent, her gold mane flying.

"We've been so anxious, girls," she said. "But when the air cleared we knew you'd found Shimmerbreeze's locket. Well done!"

Before the girls could reply, there was a distant rumbling. Emily, Aisha and the unicorns watched in horror as the sky darkened and a black cloud rolled towards them. The rumbling grew louder. The cloud boiled overhead, fizzing with daggers of electricity.

"Oh no!" cried Aisha. "Selena's back!"

Chapter Eight
Sky Dance

The black cloud suddenly burst and
Selena stood before them. Lightning bolts
shot from her horn, making the grass
sizzle where they hit. The locket around
her neck shook with the fierce storm
that raged inside. Flit flew above her,
chattering nervously.

Selena fixed Emily and Aisha with a furious glare.

"You think you're so clever," she snarled. "But you're foolish if you think you can beat me. One day soon, the kingdom will be mine, and everyone will bow down before Queen Selena."

"Not while we're here to stop you," Aisha declared.

"Stop me?" Selena's eyes blazed. "No one is going to stop me. Don't forget I've still got two of the precious lockets. I *will* be queen of Enchanted Valley!"

With a cackle and a final stamp of her hooves she launched herself into the air and flew off in a swirl of black cloud.

"You'd better watch out!" twittered Flit. "Selena always wins. She'll be back!"

"FLIT!" Selena screeched at him. Flit gave a yelp and swooped away.

When they had disappeared into the clouds, Aurora bent her beautiful head to Emily and Aisha. "Don't listen to her," she said. "She's just a bad loser. You've saved our kingdom again. I don't know what we'd have done without you. Now you must enjoy the rest of your visit here."

"Let's fly some kites!" suggested Shimmerbreeze.

Aisha chose a sky-blue kite decorated with silver moons. Emily's was star-shaped and had yellow ribbon streamers.

Emily frowned. "But these kites haven't got strings. How can we fly them?"

Shimmerbreeze gave her a wink, then looked at the kites. Her horn began to glow silver and the clouds inside her locket glimmered and twirled. At once, the two kites soared into the air. Shimmerbreeze waved her horn, and the kites bobbed round each other as they weaved back and forth in the sky.

"Now you try," said Shimmerbreeze.

The girls each moved a hand through the air, and the kites copied what they were doing.

Aisha made her kite fly in a figure of eight, while Emily made hers skim over the trees, sending the lanterns swinging.

"Wow!" cried both girls.

All of a sudden, a host of pink butterflies rose from the branches and joined in the merry sky dance. Aurora watched, her eyes twinkling with delight.

"Like you in the tornado!" said Emily.

"I don't think I was as graceful as those butterflies," Aisha laughed.

At last the sun began to dip below the faraway mountains, covering the valley in a warm glow like candlelight.

"Can you hear that?" asked Emily.

Aisha listened. A sweet song was drifting towards them on the evening breeze:

**Goodnight sun,
Hello moon,
Goodbye day,
See you soon.**

"Ember and her chicks are singing a lullaby together," said Aurora softly.

Emily and Aisha smiled at each other. The phoenixes sounded content – and very sleepy.

Aisha gave a great yawn.

"I think it's time for us to go home," said Emily. They ran to each of the unicorns, giving them a big hug goodbye.

Aurora gently touched her muzzle to their cheeks. "Enchanted Valley is sure to need your help again," she said. "After all, there are two more stolen lockets to find."

"You can count on us," said Aisha.

"We won't let Selena win," Emily added, nodding.

Queen Aurora swished her horn above their heads. A warm mist of golden sparkles surrounded them, and before they could blink they were back in the garden of Aisha's cottage. No time had passed while they were in the magical realm.

Aisha looked at the phoenix statue.

"It looks just like Ember," she said.

Emily nodded. "I bet she's having fun with her little chicks!" she said. "What an amazing adventure we had."

"Look, Emily," gasped Aisha.

A single cloud was moving lazily over the cottage.

"It has four legs!" said Emily.

"And a mane," said Aisha.

"And a spiral horn!" cried Emily. "It's a unicorn!" They hugged each other tightly.

"Maybe it's a sign," whispered Aisha. "A sign that we'll be seeing our friends again very soon."

"I hope so," said Emily with a big grin. "I can't wait for another unicorn adventure!"

The End

Join Emily and Aisha
for another adventure in …
Glitterhoof's
Secret Garden
Read on for a sneak peek!

Rain pattered hard against the windows of Enchanted Cottage.

"I don't think we'll be playing football today," said Aisha Khan with a sigh. She and her best friend, Emily Turner, were watching the rain from the warm kitchen. Drops fell from the flowers in the garden, and trickled over the wings of the phoenix statue in the middle of the lawn.

"Don't worry," Emily said with a grin. "I know what we can do instead!"

Aisha smiled back. "A science experiment?"

"How did you guess?" Emily laughed.
She loved science as much as Aisha loved
sport. "First we need some flowers …"

The two girls darted out of the back
door into the wet garden. They hadn't
known each other long, as Aisha and her
parents had only recently moved into
Enchanted Cottage. But already they did
everything together – and they had even
shared some magical adventures …

The girls picked a handful of flowers.
Then they ran back indoors, shaking rain
from their hair.

Soon Aisha's mum had helped the girls
set up their experiment. On the kitchen
table were several small bowls of water,
with a few drops of food colouring in

each one. The girls put the flowers in the coloured water.

"What happens now?" asked Aisha.

"Wait and see," said Emily with a smile. The two girls drank hot chocolate and chatted with Mrs Khan, who was stirring a saucepan of curry on the stove.

After a while, Mrs Khan pointed at the flowers. "Girls, look!"

Aisha gasped. The flowers were changing colour! The yellow petals were turning blue and the pink petals were turning green.

"They're drinking up the food colouring," Emily explained with a grin.

Aisha peered closely at some white petals, now edged with pink. "It's almost like magic," she whispered.

Emily knew they were both thinking about the same thing – Enchanted Valley, the magical realm they had visited, which was filled with unicorns and other amazing creatures!

Read
Glitterhoof's Secret Garden
to find out what adventures are in store for Aisha and Emily!

Also available

Book One:

Dawnblaze Saves Summer

Book Two:

Shimmerbreeze & the Sky Spell

Book Three:

Glitterhoof's Secret Garden

Book Four:

Sparklesplash Meets the Mermaids

Look out for the next book!

If you like
Unicorn Magic,
you'll love ...

Welcome to Animal Ark!

Animal-mad Amelia is sad
about moving house, until she
discovers Animal Ark, where vets look
after all kinds of animals in need.

Join Amelia and her friend Sam for a
brand-new series of animal adventures!